D1272599

-My Family-
My Special Needs Family

by Claudia Harrington
illustrated by Zoe Persico

Looking Glass Library

An Imprint of Magic Wagon
abdopublishing.com

Special thanks to: Tess Kallmeyer, LMSW and Jenna Roberts, MD —CH

To my family dogs for always giving me dog kisses and nice strolls in the park. I miss you every day Lacey. —ZP

abdopublishing.com

Published by Magic Wagon, a division of ABDO, PO Box 398166, Minneapolis, Minnesota 55439. Copyright © 2018 by Abdo Consulting Group, Inc. International copyrights reserved in all countries. No part of this book may be reproduced in any form without written permission from the publisher. Looking Glass Library™ is a trademark and logo of Magic Wagon.

Printed in the United States of America, North Mankato, Minnesota.
052017
092017

Written by Claudia Harrington
Illustrated by Zoe Persico
Edited by Heidi M.D. Elston
Art Directed by Candice Keimig

Publisher's Cataloging-in-Publication Data

Names: Harrington, Claudia, author. | Persico, Zoe, illustrator.
Title: My special needs family / by Claudia Harrington ; illustrated by Zoe Persico.
Description: Minneapolis, MN : Magic Wagon, 2018. | Series: My family
Summary: Lenny follows Roxy for a school project and learns about a classmate with special needs.
Identifiers: LCCN 2017930506 | ISBN 9781532130212 (lib. bdg.) | ISBN 9781614798361 (ebook) | ISBN 9781614798439 (Read-to-me ebook)
Subjects: LCSH: Family--Juvenile fiction. | Family life--Juvenile fiction. | Autism--Juvenile fiction.
Classification: DDC [E]--dc23
LC record available at http://lccn.loc.gov/2017930506

When the school day ended, Miss Fish said good-bye to her second graders.

"Lenny, wait! You're going home with Roxy. She's Student of the Week!"

"Cool," said Lenny.

Click!

"How do you get home?" asked Lenny.

"Mom picks me up at ten after three," said Roxy.

"Great," said Lenny.

"Hop in, kids," said Roxy's mom.
Click!

Roxy's mom drove them to a bowling alley.

"Wow!" said Lenny. "We get to bowl?"

"I have to practice," said Roxy.

Lenny's ball bounced down the gutter.

"That's not the right way," said Roxy. She bowled a strike.

Click!

Lenny whooped. "Steee-rike! Who taught you to bowl?"

"My dad gives lessons," said Roxy.

"Cool," said Lenny. His ball flew into the next lane. "Maybe he could give me one."

Roxy watched the ball roll slowly.

"Please answer Lenny," said Roxy's mom.

"Maybe I need two," said Lenny. He cracked up.

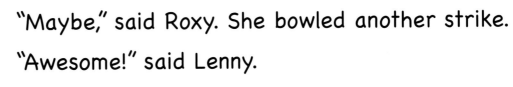

"Maybe," said Roxy. She bowled another strike.

"Awesome!" said Lenny.

Roxy's mom cheered. After a few more turns, she said, "Time to go home, you two."

Soon they pulled into Roxy's driveway.

Click!

Lenny's stomach growled.

"Was that noise you?" asked Roxy.

Lenny blushed. "I must be hungry. Who gets your snack?"

"Welcome, Lenny," said Roxy's mom when they went in. "Roxy, show Lenny the snack chart."

Roxy pointed to a chart on the refrigerator.

A dog nosed Roxy's leg.

"You have a dog?" asked Lenny.

"Yes," answered Roxy.

"Tell Lenny what her name is," said Roxy's mom.

"Dog," Roxy said.

Dog nudged Lenny.
Click!

"I do snacks. It's carrots and apples today. Now we wash our hands."

After their snack, Roxy checked the clock. "At 4:45 p.m., it's homework."

"Who helps?" asked Lenny.

"My mom," said Roxy. "Dad gets home later. I'm going to bowl in the hall now."

"Roxy, ask Lenny if he wants to bowl, too," said her mom.

"Want to bowl?" Roxy asked.

"Really?" asked Lenny. "I don't want to wreck your house."

"They're foam," said Roxy.

Click!

When they'd each had a turn, Roxy checked the time.

Then she ran to the kitchen.

Dog trotted behind.

"Mom! Homework!"

When their worksheets were done, Roxy looked at the clock.

"What time will Dad get home?"

"Five thirty," said her mom.

"What time will Dad get home?" Roxy asked again.

Her mom smiled. "Roxy, you need to think about the answer I gave you the first time."

Roxy grabbed a carrot. "I'm eating more carrots!"

"Snack time is over," said her mom.

Dog whined.

Soon, Roxy's dad walked in. Roxy leaped into his arms.

"Hello, family. And you must be Lenny," he said.

Click!

"Hi," Lenny said.

"Come see my room," said Roxy, starting down the hall.

Dog followed.

When they got to her room, Roxy beamed.

"Wow!" said Lenny. "Are all these trophies yours?"

Click!

"Yes," said Roxy. "They're from Special Olympics!"

"Cool," said Lenny. "Who keeps them so shiny?"

Roxy dusted a trophy and put a gold star on the wall chart. "I do."

Did you clean your room?

1st

2nd

#1

1st

Roxy checked the clock and ran to the hall.

"What's up?" asked Lenny.

Roxy waited.

"Dinner!" called her dad.

Dog took off toward the kitchen.

Lenny smiled. "Who makes it?"

"Mom, usually. Dad only knows bowling alley food."

Lenny laughed.

When they finished their chicken piccata, the doorbell rang.

"Not yet!" said Lenny as his mom came in. "I still have more questions. Who cleans up?"

"Everybody," said Roxy.

"Even Dog," added her mom.

Click!

"Can I help, Mom?" asked Lenny.

His mom smiled. "Yes, but be quick."

Popping the last suds bubble, Lenny asked, "Who tucks you in at bedtime?"

Roxy yawned. "Mom and Dad both."

"Speaking of bedtime . . ." her mom said.

"I know," said Roxy, checking the time.

"Before I go," said Lenny, "who loves you best?"

Roxy's parents hugged her as Lenny's mom kissed the top of his head.

"We do!" they all said.

Dog slurped Roxy a giant kiss.

Click!

Student of the Week

Roxy

"See you tomorrow, bowling champ!" said Lenny, following his mom out.

"Okay," said Roxy.